# One Boy,
## One dream,
### One club...

Arsenal?

Man U?

Everton?

Chelsea?

Villa?

Leeds?

# E.R.Reilly

FIRST
STEP

PUBLISHED IN GREAT BRITAIN BY
FIRST STEP
PO BOX 8808
BIRMINGHAM
B30 2LR
E-mail (for orders and enquiries):
firststep@reilly19.freeserve.co.uk

© E.R.Reilly 2001

First published in 2001 under a nom de plume

Reprinted 2001, 2002, 2003, 2005, 2007

ISBN 0-9539229-2-8

Printed and bound by OM Authentic Media,
P O Box 2014
Secunderabad 500 003
Andhra Pradesh, India
Tel: 040-27861151/ 27861152

Very special thanks to
Jean for everything!

We all have talent. The lucky ones know it.

## Prologue

*The book you have just started reading is one of the most important fictions of our time. It is important because the person that it is about is very famous. His name is known by almost every person in the country. His story is very special indeed because his life was far from easy, but he managed to overcome any hurdles that came before him because he is, and has always been, single-minded. He knew what he wanted from a very young age. There was only ever one thing that he wanted to do with his life and that was to play football. There was only ever one club that he ever wanted to play for and that was Manchester United. His was a dream that was more than a fancy. He came from good stock. His father showed early promising signs of becoming a professional footballer but his career was cut short by injury before it had really begun.*

*You might well ask why this story isn't well known already. The truth is that there are a few skeletons in the cupboard and* telling the whole truth in a normal biography would be unfair to his family. Also there are some behind-the-scenes dealings that used to go on in football that would cause a lot of trouble if they were to come out in the open today. This would clearly cause a lot of embarrassment to the subject of this book, but it would also cause a lot of embarrassment to the football club concerned as well. Some of the shady dealings that are exposed in this book still go on today but, in fairness to the club involved, and the game as a whole, it should be noted that football is a much cleaner game now.

For these reasons, the name of the person whose life is told in this book has been changed and the names of all the clubs have also been changed. Of course, there will undoubtedly be a lot of speculation about who the person is and people will try and discover the real clubs involved. This, however, will have to remain idle speculation because the person whose life this is about and indeed my own identity will remain forever a secret.

*From here on in, the name, Adam, will be used to describe my friend. Adam was my best friend at school and I'm proud to say that I was his. We were both driven by ambition that took hold of us at a very early age indeed. I look at young children now, at age six or seven, and it seems impossible, but it is true to say that Adam and I were already seriously discussing what we wanted to do in life. Like most young people I wanted to work for the police for a while, then I wanted to be a train driver and a fireman. I know that for quite a long time I wanted to be a priest. I remember talking to my own priest about it on a number of occasions and, when I was eleven, I very nearly left home to go to a college where boys study throughout their teens and then go on to train as priests. I very well may have followed that path had it not been for the fact that the college only played rugby and football was just altogether too important to me. There was no way I could have given up football. Looking back, I guess that let me know how serious my calling was. I eventually went on to choose a* career in journalism. I want to say that I have a fairly ordinary career but this book is all about the truth so I am going to suspend modesty and say that I am at the top of my profession. That's enough said about me, though, because my life's story only becomes interesting when people learn that I am Adam's best friend.

Adam went through no soul searching for his choice of career. He was certain that one day he would be a professional footballer and his overwhelming dream in life was to play for Manchester United. All of us who knew him, even as a very young boy, knew that he had a most prestigious talent and that he worked and trained harder than anyone else we knew. The problem was that we never knew how good you had to be to be a pro.

Adam's life has not been easy and the reason for this was that some people were really quite unkind to him as he was growing up. All of their names have been changed.

There was one person who stood out like a beacon in both Adam's and my life. He was our teacher from primary school. We would like to have used his real name so that we could tell the world what a brilliant teacher he was and what a wonderful inspiration he was to both of us. Unfortunately, this might give the game away as Adam has been photographed with him on a number of occasions, and once people know who he is, then the whole point of this book being written with false names would be ruined. For that reason, I will be calling the teacher John Smith. For the record though, John Smith knows who he is and Adam and I want to say that we realise that so much of our success in life has its roots back in those early days when he listened to us and took us, and our dreams, seriously. Nobody could have done more for us and we thank him from the bottom of our hearts. Even now, I see adults who make children feel foolish for having dreams. I make a point of writing in my columns that adults who do that are putting unnecessary barriers in the way of young people. Adults need to encourage young people to have dreams. They need to help them work towards their dreams. Dreams can never be realised if they are not kept alive. Once a dream fades, it dies forever. Adam would never let his dream fade and that is why I have written his story today and it is the reason you are reading it.

You can do
anything
if you try.

## Chapter One

The whole story that I am now telling you nearly didn't happen at all. On one very rare occasion when Adam and I were not playing football, we found ourselves on an adventure that nearly cost us our lives. We went on a summer holiday with Adam's mum and stepdad. The idea was that we would have a week with them and then Adam's birth father would come down and we would stop with him. We were then due to go on holiday with my parents for two weeks, so we were really as happy as we could be.

It was probably the best and worst summer of our young lives. The days started really early. We went out in the mornings and played football. Some people would say that we were training or working at our skills but really we were just playing. Sometimes you can hear the sentiment when Adam is interviewed on television. Even when he's playing with the best footballers in the world, he still describes what he does as playing. He says that if he ever feels like he's going to work, then he'll pack it in and get a real job.

We used to do things like keeping the ball in the air between us. We got so good at it that we used to see how long we could keep it going for, rather than counting how many kicks. We used to put cones down on the ground and dribble in between them. We used to time ourselves to see if we were getting better. I was pretty good at it but, of course, Adam would win every time. We used to make it a fairer contest by putting more cones on the ground on Adam's side. Target practice was something that could keep us busy for hours and hours and hours. Adam's free kicks today are recognised by most people as being the best in the world. People are staggered to learn that he spent so many hours practising them from such an early age. I know the truth though – it was simply playing. He did have the desire to be the best footballer that he could be, and there was some inner strength that has always kept him going, but really the plain truth is that we just played football from early in the morning until late at night because we loved it.

Adam's mum and stepdad called us in at about mid-morning but by then we had already been playing football for about three hours. We went down to the seaside to spend the rest of the day there. The idea was that Adam's dad would come to meet us and we would swap over. His mum and stepdad would then go off home and we would stay on holiday for another week with Adam's dad. It was quite a busy beach and we soon found some other kids to play with. We rigged up a little net and played kick volleyball.

The other kids couldn't understand why we were so good at it but it was the kind of thing that we did for hours every day so we had something of an advantage. We could see that people were gathering round us to watch us keep the ball up. We loved being the centre of attention. I suppose people wouldn't have taken much notice but we were still at primary school so it stood out that our skill levels were so high. Of course, it was Adam that was really good. He made it easy for me to control the ball because he kept it under such good control. I never had to reach out or run for the ball. It always came just where I wanted it.

Adam's stepdad never really liked Adam. He was like two different people. When there was nobody else around he used to order Adam about and shout at him. He would punish him for the smallest thing. I am absolutely convinced that he treated Adam so badly because he was jealous. Adam's stepfather and his real father didn't get along. Adam's dad was really good at football and I think that's what his stepdad didn't like. He used to pretend to be proud of Adam and when other people were around he would say encouraging things, but that's where it stopped. He would never say or do anything supportive in private.

When he could see the crowd gathered around us on the beach, he shouted over to Adam and told him to stop showing off. He said it in a kind of joking voice with a smile on his face, but I could tell he was jealous. He would have loved to have been the centre of attention himself. As the crowd was getting bigger and people were clapping more, Adam was showing off more. When a high ball came, he kind of caught it on the back of his neck and balanced it there. He had a big smile on his face. He wasn't a big head but he loved to make people happy and he did always like to show off his skills. His stepdad clearly wasn't as happy as he pretended to be and so he called to us again and told us to come over for our sandwiches.

Adam always did what he was told first time where his stepfather was concerned because he knew what the consequences would be if he didn't. Everybody gave us a big round of applause. Adam kicked the ball over to where his mum and stepdad were sitting and that's when the whole day started to go wrong. Adam's stepdad said that he had kicked sand all over the sandwiches. He hadn't. I saw exactly what happened and there was definitely no sand anywhere near any piece of food. I didn't say anything because I knew that the angrier his stepdad became, the more trouble Adam would get into. Adam's stepdad picked up a knife and stuck it into the ball. He whispered into Adam's ear that it would be a good idea if he went and played out of his sight whilst he tried to salvage something from the picnic.

We went off and wandered down to another part of the beach. I never thought much about Adam's mum at the time but, now I look back, I think she should have stood up for him more. We didn't bother going back for lunch. We just started messing about on the beach and gradually forgot about Adam's stepdad.

It was a beautiful summer's day. We wrestled for a while, trying to pin each other's shoulders to the ground. We used to do that quite a lot when we were very young but we never hurt each other. I was stronger and bigger than Adam but I could play wrestle with him for ages without ever hurting him.

We found an old tray and played sand surfing on it. There was a steep embankment of sand and we ran up it as fast as we could. We flew down the sand on that old tray and fell over at the bottom of the slope. I remember it being very hard work but it was great fun so we just kept on doing it again and again.

There was a family nearby who were packing away for the day and we invited the kids to come and join us. They were a boy and girl just a bit older than us. We had competitions with them to see who could go the furthest or to see who could do the most spectacular dive as we came off.

It was a good afternoon. As the family were leaving, they gave us two dinghies because they were too big to fit in the car. It was like a dream come true for us. If we couldn't play football, then being around in the water seemed like a good second best.

Adam's dad turned up. We were quite a long way from him and we now had the dinghies in tow so we just waved over to him and he waved back. We saw him sit down next to Adam's mum so we just carried on playing for a while. We dragged the dinghies out into the water and just lay back in the still water soaking up the sun. The water lapped quietly around us. It was blissfully peaceful. It was a wonderful feeling to know that Adam's dad was going to be with us for the next week.

It wasn't that we did anything different with Adam's dad; in fact, we didn't really do anything with him at all. He was a bit of an invalid. He could get around a bit, but he moved very slowly. He had metal crutches that he used if he was walking from the house to the car but he just used a stick when he was walking around the house.

If we closed our eyes for a bit, we drifted apart so we held onto each other's dinghy. There's something about water; it is more peaceful being on it than being anywhere else. We chatted about anything that came into our heads, but football usually came into every conversation we ever had. We talked about matches that we had been in and matches that we were going to be in and always we talked about Manchester United. Man.U., Man.U., Man.U., Adam was obsessed by Man.U. He always talked about Man.U. as though they were his team. He said that he was going to play for them one day. He said it with such conviction that I believed him. Most people either ignored him or poked fun at him. That was unless they really knew him. If they really knew him, then they would know how much inner strength he had and how determined he was.

We heard his dad whistle to us from the shore. We looked over to him. He was waving at us and we waved back. I think I liked his dad nearly as much as Adam did.

We just lay back doing "chilli beans". That's what we said when we were taking it easy. We decided to stay in the water for a while so we didn't have to talk to Adam's stepdad. We knew that we would have to come and say goodbye when they were leaving, but we decided to wait until we were called for. We just drifted around, chatting and enjoying the end to a beautiful day.

I didn't want to make Adam go back until he was ready, but I was getting hungry. We had been out playing since seven o'clock that morning and we hadn't had anything to eat. We had skipped breakfast because we were too busy playing football and we missed lunch because Adam's stepdad was throwing one of his wobbly moods, so I asked Adam if he minded going back and he was cool about it. The sun had gone down anyway. It was a warm evening but it was time to go and get something to eat.

We started to row with our hands. We lay down on our tummies and kind of half rowed and half swam. We had drifted quite far out so we had to get a move on. I got quite far in front of Adam because I was a stronger swimmer but he called me back because he was getting a bit scared. I understood because we were quite a way out. I waited for him to catch up. It did take

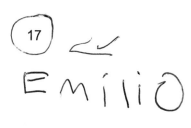

him quite a while to catch up so I promised that I would slow down and wait for him. We took a little breather and started again. I tried to go slowly so that I didn't get separated from him, but if I didn't go quite so fast I didn't seem to get anywhere. I took a few minutes going forward slowly, and then waited a minute or so for Adam to catch up. I did this a few times until I realised that we were actually further away now than when we had started back.

When Adam caught up with me I told him that we would have to really get a move on because the tide was taking us out to sea. It was no use, though. He had already been trying as hard as he could and he was getting nowhere. We discussed the possibility of me going on alone and raising the alarm with the coast guard so that they could come and save Adam. Adam was clearly very frightened and didn't want to be left alone so I stayed with him. We decided to have an out and out push for home. I went in front and we did the same as we did before. I would stop after about ten minutes and then shout back to Adam to encourage him to keep up. It was hopeless, though. We were just getting more and more tired and further and further out to sea.

Adam was all but exhausted. For some strange reason I didn't feel quite as bad as him. Adam couldn't apologise enough but looking back on it now it was probably hypothermia and exhaustion that made him so tired. I remember drinking some pop on the beach but I don't think that Adam stopped for any food or drink all day and as it was such a warm day it's a wonder we didn't both pass out.

We decided to abandon Adam's dinghy so that we could both work together to make it easier to get back. This was the biggest mistake that we made. When we were both in the dinghy, it sank really low in the water. It was so low that we couldn't make it go forward at all. We watched helplessly as Adam's dinghy drifted away. Within a minute it was virtually out of sight and that's when we realised we were in real danger. Until then we hadn't really realised how fast we were drifting out to sea. We had been reluctant to shout for help because we were embarrassed, but now all thoughts of embarrassment left us as we started shouting and screaming for help. We could still hear a murmur of voices on the beach but we couldn't make any of the voices out nor could we see whether Adam's mum and stepdad were still there.

We never panicked because we knew it could only be a matter of time before Adam's parents raised the alarm and the coast guard would come and get us. Fear does have a habit of controlling your mind, though, if you let it. The night air grew colder and the shoreline gradually became a haze of distant lights and far off fairground sounds. We could hear people laughing and shouting in the distance. It was somehow reassuring. The hunger, the thirst and the cold made us quiet. We talked about being saved rather than of dying. It was a scary time. As the night grew darker, we couldn't understand why Adam's parents hadn't raised the alarm.

Then it occurred to us that Adam's mum and stepdad could be waiting for us and so could Adam's dad. If each thought we were with the other, neither would raise the alarm. This was a disaster.

Eventually a plane flew overhead. It was a wonderful relief. We cheered and shouted and raised our hands and waved like mad, but relief turned to disappointment as the plane flew on overhead and away. It seemed a very long time that we stayed aimlessly bobbing about until we eventually noticed something sticking up out of the water. It was a fisherman's net. There was a kind of post that held it still in the water. We drifted near to it but it looked like we were going to float just by it and yet be unable to grasp it. We could see the net floating around near it so I jumped out and swam a few metres and caught hold of it. I swam back to Adam and he paddled like mad to stay in touch with me.

We held on to that post as though it were the hand of God. We knew that as long as we held onto it, we only had to stay alive until the morning when the fishermen came to check their catch to be saved. A helicopter flew overhead and, once again, we screamed and shouted. Our spirits were raised even higher than before because the helicopter had a searchlight. It came tantalisingly close to us on a number of occasions, but, even when it appeared to shine its light directly on us, it didn't actually lower a winch for us. We found out later that, even though they had spotted us, they couldn't risk capsizing our flimsy dinghy by getting too close to it. It wasn't long before a speedboat came out to get us and we were rescued at last.

That was a life changing experience for me and I know that it was for Adam. We learnt how precious life is and we learnt not to take it for granted.

We were right about Adam's mum and stepdad. They had agreed for Adam's dad to pick us up and take us to where we had been stopping to collect our things. When he got to the beach and saw that we had already gone, he stormed off in a huff back to his hotel. He had decided that Adam's mum should deliver us to him as a punishment for messing him about. When Adam's dad didn't turn up at his mum's caravan, she eventually went over to his hotel room to find out the reason why he hadn't turned up. That is when they raised the alarm.

To this day, Adam's parents blame each other for the whole sorry mess but I blame both of them. If they had both put Adam first, instead of their own stupid squabbles, then none of it would have happened.

They say that every cloud has a silver lining, though, and that day was the day that really cemented our friendship. We had always been best friends but from that day on we became lifelong best friends.

# Practice only works when it is FUN!

## Chapter Two

I want you to know Adam the man, but to do this you really need to know Adam the boy. I know that many people say that when they were children they wanted to be ballerinas or professional footballers or spacemen or any number of other wonderful things but few people think this at a very early age and really mean it.

Adam had a diary and he wrote in it every week. He used to keep writing Man.U., Man.U., over and over again. I know why he did it. Other people used to tease him because he talked about Man.U. so much. I never did. I was fascinated by him and his dreams. Writing Man.U. all the time used to help him meet the need he had to keep reminding himself that he was working towards his dream.

He started his diary when he was seven but it was sometime later that he started writing in it every week. One of his earliest entries was, *"Man.U., Man.U.,*

*Man.U., I just KNOW that I will play for Man.U. one day"*.

He didn't share his diary with anybody except me. Now, of course, he can be proud of being so determined and single minded but at the time he knew that people would laugh at him even if they knew how good he was at football.

The real purpose of his diary was for Adam to keep a record of what he had actually done to help himself get nearer to his dream. He wrote things like, *"one day I will be selected to play for Manchester United. I will be handed the shirt (with my name on it!) by the manager and he will shake my hand. That's where I am going and this is what I have done to help myself get there."* Then he would make a list of all the games he had played and the training he had done.

We had a game that we played for hours almost every day of our lives. We never gave it a name but it was a kind of target practice game. Each of us took a shot at a sign that was on a wall. If we hit it, we scored a point and if we missed it, then we didn't score. It was a good game because we had to decide whether to take an early shot from near the target or to let the ball come to rest and then take a dead ball shot. I didn't find out until much later that Adam used to keep a record of his scores. If he improved upon his previous best, then he would record in his diary that he was one step nearer his dream. It makes me smile to look back on those days now but at the time the irony of it totally escaped us, because the sign that we spent all those hours trying to hit said "NO BALL GAMES".

Adam still has his diaries from those early days and we noticed one day, when we were looking through them, that from one year to the next we could count on the fingers of one hand the number of entries that didn't mention football.

It was Adam's diary that started another memorable incident from our childhood. You may think that a boy who is a very gifted footballer would automatically become very popular at school but in Adam's case that was very far from the truth. Not only was Adam not very popular at school, he was actually quite unpopular. Quite a lot of boys didn't like him because he was so good at football and some boys, especially ones who wanted to be the best themselves, actually hated him. It wasn't unusual for Adam to experience a bit of teasing or even a bit of bullying from time to time.

A particularly cruel incident started one day with some boys who were sitting at the back of the class. They were putting their heads together with some of the girls and they were sniggering and laughing. They kept looking over at Adam so it was obvious that they were making fun of him in some way. We took no notice. It wasn't a one-off incident so we had learnt to deal with it. If we could ignore that kind of thing then we would. I shouldn't really be proud of this but I'm afraid I am; if it ever came to a fight, then nine times out of ten it would be me that would stand in and fight in Adam's stead. The sniggering and laughing continued and we kept on ignoring it.

In the lesson that followed, the class was asked to come up with a sentence with the word "love" in it. One of the boys from the back of the class put his hand up and said, "Man.U. Oh, Man.U., I love you. I love you Man.U."

The group of kids at the back burst out laughing. At this stage, we didn't think too much about it. Later in the day, though, we walked into a classroom and someone had written on the chalkboard, "I kept the ball up for seventeen minutes today so it's obvious that I'm going to be playing for Man.U." Then they had signed it "Adam". Everybody went quiet and stared at Adam. I can only guess how hurt he was. It was obvious that somebody had got hold of his diary and had been reading it out loud to everybody in the class.

I could see Adam fighting back his tears but it was no use. His emotions got the better of him and his tears flowed freely. He wasn't showing any other signs of emotion. His face was straight but his tears took no notice of his efforts and just flooded his face. One of the girls said, "Ahhh! Is little Adam crying then?"

The humiliation and the embarrassment were too much for him. He ran from the room.

Adam ran out of school, but nobody knew this at the time. I told our Mr Smith what had happened. Mr Smith was the one great adult in our school lives. He stood out like a beacon among all the other teachers. The influence he had on our young lives was massive. He came in and, although he was really nice, he was one of those teachers that nobody messed about. He burst into the room with all guns blazing. He started fiercely telling all of the class how disappointed he was that they should stoop so low. He asked them how they would feel if their innermost thoughts had been laid open to ridicule for everyone to laugh at. By the time he had finished, he had made them feel really guilty. I could tell that some of the kids realised how cruel they had been. I could also see that some of the kids didn't have the faintest idea of how bad Adam felt.

Mr Smith told the class that everyone who had been involved was as guilty as the person who had started it. He also told them that he was determined to find out who stole the diary and punish whoever it was. Mr Smith was one of those people that, when they said something, you just knew that they really meant it. He found out that it was a lad called Michael Jones who had stolen the diary. Michael, more than any other boy in the school, really disliked Adam. Michael was a good footballer. He was a very good footballer, to be honest, but he wasn't a patch on Adam.

Everything changes with time. I used to hate Michael when we were at school. Looking back now, I can see how hard it was for him. Football was very important to him, but all through his school life he had to put up with Adam being so much better. In most schools, Michael would have been the best player, but in our school, everything he achieved was eclipsed by Adam's achievements. If Michael scored three goals, Adam would score six. If Michael was picked for the district team, Adam was picked for the county. Now I know how hard it must have been for him, but at the time all I could see was a jealous, cruel bully who made my best friend's life a misery.

Mr Smith did punish Michael. He made him write a letter of apology to Adam and he put him on detention. He also banned Michael from playing for the school's team. It was a few days later that Adam found out about this and did something I couldn't understand at the time. When he found out what Mr Smith had done, he asked him to allow Michael to play for the school team. It is not my intention to make Adam out to be whiter than white but that really was the way it happened. Mr Smith allowed Michael to play for the team but Michael never found out that it was Adam who had spoken up for him.

Apart from Adam himself, I was the only person in the world that knew just how embarrassed Adam was and how much this incident had upset him. To this day, Adam impresses me most when he's not trying to impress. That small act of kindness may not have made him a saint, but I think it was a pointer to show just what a good kid he was.

Michael did write the letter of apology, but he didn't mean it. Adam and I disliked him with a passion but I think that his hatred for us in general, and for Adam in particular, ran much deeper. This was far from being the only time that Michael was vindictive to Adam, but I think this incident hurt Adam the most. I think if he had been a bit older then it wouldn't have hurt him so much. There are two reasons that make me think this: one reason is that Adam's dream of playing for Manchester United was, at this stage, still a very private one, and the other reason is that people hadn't yet come to realise just how talented Adam was.

When this happened, Adam ran out of school. It was quite a bit later when the teachers realised that he was missing. They rang his mum, but he wasn't there, so they rang his dad and he wasn't there either. This was a cue for his mum and dad to start blaming each other and to start screaming abuse at each other. Because he had been gone so long, the school called the police. Some of the teachers went looking for him; his mum went looking for him too. His dad couldn't get around too well, so he stayed by the phone in case Adam called home.

The teachers came and questioned me. They asked me where Adam might have gone. The police came as well; they asked me the same questions but I told them nothing. As soon as the attention drifted away from me, I went to see him. I knew exactly where he would be. We had a secret den that we went to when it was too dark to play football. There were some gully ways that ran behind the back streets of our estate and we had built a lean-to up against the back of some garage walls. It was surrounded by hedges and mounds of earth. We had put some camouflage of our own around it so that nobody knew it was there except us. People could walk just a few metres away from it and not know it was there.

We sat quietly. We didn't need to talk. After a while, I told him that it was Michael Jones that had stolen the diary. Adam wasn't surprised. I told him that the police were looking for him. He was surprised about that. I told him that it was the other kids who should feel ashamed and not he. He said that he wasn't ashamed, he just felt stupid and betrayed. We eventually went home. He knew that his stepdad would give him a hard time, but he didn't care.

I'm a bit in awe of Adam. I still hang on his every word – even today. A while ago, I heard him say in an interview that, when people face up to tough times and overcome them, it just makes them tougher. I'm sure he wouldn't have been able to say that at the time but I'm sure that's when he learnt it.

You know
that you
have done
well when
you feel
good.

## Chapter Three

If I were to write about my own family life as I was growing up, it would be a lot better than Adam's. The thing is, though, that I would make a point of only writing nice things about my parents. There would be no point in writing about all of the bad things that I could remember. It would only upset people. The point of this story, though, is to try to explain that Adam had the kind of childhood that he could easily use as an excuse for not doing well in life. Adam would never make excuses, though. If he didn't practise playing football for a day, he wouldn't make any excuses. He would just accept it and then go out and work twice as hard the next day.

How he came to be like this is something of a mystery. It certainly wasn't as a result of watching good rôle models. I must say that his mother never went out of her way to be cruel to him. She was a fairly run-of-the-mill kind of mum but she didn't go out of her way to stop his stepdad being cruel to him either. I have tried to think of some positive things to say about Adam's stepfather but really my memory of him is that, like Michael Jones, he was a cruel, vindictive, jealous bully. In order to be as impartial as I possibly can, I would say that the best thing about him is that he was well liked by his friends. He was always laughing and joking whenever he was in company. It was just where Adam was concerned, and in private, that he would become a real tyrant who would pick on his stepson for little or no reason.

I'll give you a couple of examples of the way he used to treat Adam. There was one time when he banned Adam from playing football and grounded him for a week. I can't remember what Adam was supposed to have done wrong, but it didn't take much. He knew how much it hurt Adam not to play football and that's why he did it. On this occasion, Adam stayed in his room every night when he got home from school but usually, when he was grounded, he would still play in the evenings. His mum would let him go out to play as long as he was back before his stepdad and they both pretended he had been home the whole time. As his stepdad was home on this occasion he had to stay in his room.

Adam had a big picture of himself on his bedroom wall. It was a newspaper cutting from the local paper. It was a picture of him holding up the cup that his team had won at the end of the previous season. Adam spent every evening drawing a Man.U. shirt with his name on it. He cut it to the exact same size as the picture and stuck it on. He made a big banner headline saying "Adam lifts the Cup for Man.U.". When his stepdad came in and saw it, he ripped it down and screwed it up. He told Adam that he was just a little boy who played for a little team who had won a little cup and he shouldn't get ideas above himself.

On another occasion, Adam had won the Player of the Year for his club and he was invited to a special occasion to be presented with his trophy. Adam's stepdad deliberately planned a family outing at the same time. This was one of the first big awards that Adam had won and, because he couldn't go, I had to collect it on his behalf. This, of course, took a lot of the joy out of it for Adam.

To understand Adam's childhood, you really need to understand his family as a whole. When Adam's dad was a teenager he used to hang out with a group of friends. He was a bit of a star amongst the group because he was a really good footballer.

Adam's mum had gone out with a boy who eventually became Adam's stepdad. She went out with him a few times before she started going out with Adam's dad. After a number of years, Adam's mum and dad got married and Adam was born but some time later his mum started seeing her old boyfriend again. He became Adam's stepdad.

In this day and age, it seems all too common to hear of such stories and many families cope and live with their situation really well, but, in the case of Adam's family, it was much more complicated than that. Adam's dad had successfully completed some extended trials for Manchester United. There were a number of young men who were in the same position. They all had to wait for a few weeks or a month or two to see which of them would be offered professional contracts. To be in this position must have been a wonderful thing for a young man. When you are that close to playing for a top club like Manchester United, everybody wants to be your friend. Well, nearly everybody does. Some people got very jealous indeed and it was at this time that Adam's dad and the man who was later to become his stepdad had a big falling out.

During that summer of waiting, Adam's dad joined in a friendly game of football at his local park. It wasn't an official game on a pitch with goal posts and a referee. It was just some local lads who put their bags down for goal posts and were having a kick about. That game was to be the game that changed his life forever. The grass was uneven and, as he went to kick the ball, he kicked the earth instead. The result was that he damaged his knee so badly that he would never kick a ball again.

In that instant, the whole focus of his life changed. His identity changed with it. No longer was he the young hopeful with a glittering career as a professional footballer ahead of him. From that moment on he became the man who used crutches to get around and who needed help getting in and out of cars.

I can't, in fairness, lay all the blame for Adam's unhappy childhood with his mum and stepdad. His father was a bitter man. He felt sorry for himself and he became so that he never had a good word for anybody. He had a few jobs but he never kept them for very long. He drank far too much and he gambled. It seemed to us, as children, that everything about his life was unhappy; everything except Adam, that is. Adam was the one true light that kept him from living in a void of darkness.

The bitterness between the two men, and indeed between Adam's mum and his dad, was, and still is, quite dreadful.

Adam often had quite a hard time of it at his dad's house, especially if his dad had been drinking. He still saw it as something of a refuge, though, as he hated his stepdad so much.

There was one redeeming adult figure in Adam's life and that was Mr Smith. He was everything that two boys could ask for in a teacher and much more besides. He told us that we could do anything that we wanted to do in our lives and that we could be anything that we wanted to be. He was our PE teacher but he was much more besides. He was our mentor. He would never let us say that we couldn't do something. He would make us say, "At this moment in time, I can't do this, but with hard work and determination I can do anything." He came into school early to do training sessions and he did extra training sessions every night after school.

Adam and I played for lots of teams. During the football season we could easily play four games every week. Each team thought that we only played for them. We had to pretend that we were only playing once or twice a week because there was a big push on at the time to try and stop young children from playing too much football. The authorities were worried that we would injure ourselves if we played too much. The truth is we were very fit and we loved football. We just loved it. We couldn't get enough of it. If we could have found a way, we would have played every day of our lives. The idea that we should pace ourselves in any way seemed ridiculous to us. I have since changed my mind though. I agree with the authorities. I have seen too many young boys injure themselves by playing too much football before they were fully grown. The technical term for the most common injured area is "*epithelial growth platelets*". Of course, it would have been a waste of time to try and explain that to a young boy like Adam. If a boy is absolutely football mad then virtually nothing will stop him playing.

Mr Smith took us to games for our school team and, when we both got picked for the district team, he took us to those matches also. He got us a trial for the best Saturday team in the area. This was really important because we would never have been able to get there without him. It was here that we were able to pit ourselves against the most talented players in the area. I scraped through and was offered a place in the squad. Adam was picked, of course, and went straight into the first team. He quickly became their top scorer. Before the season was out, he got picked for the older team. He was playing with boys who were up to four years older than us and he was still a star. He wasn't fazed a bit. In fact, he soon became their top scorer. You might think that this would make him the most popular boy in the team but, just like at school, there were some boys who didn't take to him. At the time I couldn't understand it but, just as with the other boys in school, I can pretty much forgive them now. It must have been a huge blow to their ego to have someone so young coming in and standing out so much. Adam often won "Man of the Match" awards. It was easy to see which of the boys was genuinely pleased for him and which boys weren't. Some gave him loud cheers and applause and they were pleased to be in the same team as someone they recognized as being an outstanding talent. Other boys either applauded very faintly or just stood with their arms folded.

Adam's dad was unable to take him to matches or training sessions. His stepdad just refused to. Mr Smith gave up his weekend regularly to ferry Adam and myself about. I never ceased to be amazed and dumbfounded at his kindness. For an adult to have given up so much of his own time to help a young boy realise his dreams was a truly wonderful act of goodwill.

I know that Adam feels just like me. Mr Smith helped both of us to enjoy our football to the full but, more importantly, he helped Adam on his first steps towards his one big dream: to play football for Manchester United.

Almost everybody who has ever realised their dreams in life will agree that taking those first early steps is the most important act. That is why both of us, and Adam in particular, owe so much to Mr Smith.

Teachers,
teach your
children to
dream.

## Chapter Four

By the age of eight, Adam was already an excellent player. By the age of nine, he was playing for an under fifteen's team. He is a man of slight build today but he was just a skinny little kid then, in all honesty. He could play football against anyone, though. No matter how big or strong his opposition were, Adam was never scared. He could give and take a tackle with the best of them. Even when older boys tried to throw their weight around, Adam would very seldom be knocked off the ball.

Adam's mum gave over the mantelpiece for his trophies. He won cups, shields and medals from the age of seven. He won individual awards such as Man of the Match, Most Valuable Player, Player of the Season and Highest Scorer. It would be false to suggest that his mum was not proud of him. She kept a scrapbook of all his newspaper cuttings as well. She just never mentioned them when his stepdad was around.

Adam's stepdad was a bit of a Jekyll and Hyde character. He was constant in his treatment of Adam but he always made out he was Adam's biggest fan whenever his friends were around. Adam's under fifteen team won through to a cup final when Adam was nine. The final was a big affair and it was being played at St Andrews, Birmingham City's ground. The league had laid on some special tickets that included a three-course meal and wine in some of the executive boxes. Adam, of course, wanted his dad to come and watch him, but things were particularly acrimonious at the time. It was Adam's weekend to be with his mum so his dad wasn't officially supposed to be there.

Adam's stepdad bought up a whole load of the executive box tickets. He wanted to show off to his friends. He had done it before. It was a disgrace to watch. He ate the expensive food at cheap prices. He got drunk on the expensive wine (that the league had paid for) and then, whenever Adam did well, all of his friends would pat him on the back and congratulate him as though he had something to do with it!

Adam told the club that he wanted a ticket for his dad but the club told him that they had already given his free ticket allocation to his stepdad. Adam tried to talk his mum into giving one of the free tickets to his dad but she didn't help him. She knew that his dad couldn't afford a ticket.

Adam and I went down to our den and just sat around for a while. He was really upset. We hatched several plans to try and find a way for Adam's dad to see the match but none of them seemed as though they would work. Adam swore to me that he wouldn't let his stepdad sit there acting the big "I am" whilst his real dad sat at home alone.

It was a big day for everyone because a day out at a big club was something of an occasion if you were football mad and it was made even more special if you knew someone who was playing. Even though it wasn't that far away, our school had organised a bus to take people to see the match. Some of the jealous boys made their excuses and didn't buy tickets but there were enough people who liked Adam and were really proud of him to fill the coach.

During the week leading up to the final, I hardly saw Adam at all. He had to train with the team every night. It was during this week that the team found out how young he was. They approached our school to see if he could have a day off to train with the others. Everybody was quite cool about it. We were worried that Mr Smith would get into trouble because he was the one who had got Adam a trial for the club in the first place. Nobody seemed very bothered, though I suppose the FA might have been, if they had found out.

When I did meet up with Adam on the night before the final, he was unusually tense. I had seen him suffer from nerves before, especially before a big match, but this time he was in quite a state. I had never seen him anywhere near as bad as this before. He was sad because his dad was going to miss the big match. I put it down to nerves. He was quiet. He drew a picture of a matchstick man on a piece of cardboard. He sat throwing darts at it across the den. He said that it was his stepdad. We walked home in virtual silence. I imagined it was me playing in the final. I had to catch my breath at just the thought of it. I remember telling him to try and sleep. He just shrugged his shoulders. I could only guess at the kind of pressure he was feeling.

I was awake a lot earlier than usual the next morning. I was the first person to arrive at school. Mr Smith arrived just after me. Adam was travelling with some people from the team. It was a beautiful sunny day in May. It was hot to be just sitting in direct sunlight. Playing in that heat would tax even the fittest professional.

As we sat waiting for the kick off, I became hopelessly nervous. I knew that Adam must have been going through torture.

The crowd grew bigger and noisier and I grew increasingly tense. The team coach was wandering around looking just about as nervous as I felt. The players were walking around the pitch. It was their last minute inspection because there was only about an hour to go before the kick off and it was time for them to go in and get changed and start stretching off.

I looked all around but I couldn't see Adam. I jokingly said to some of the other kids from school that Adam might be hugging the toilet bowl inside and throwing up with nerves. The team coach caught sight of me as he scoured the crowd. He came bounding up the steps and stooped down in front of me.

"Where is he?" he said.
"Where's Adam?" I said.
"Yes, where is he?"
"I don't know." I answered.

The coach half stamped his foot and continued to look around. He asked where Adam's mum was and when I told him, he went storming off to look for her.

I was worried in case something terrible had happened to him and he'd been run over or something.

Adam's mum and stepdad came down to where I was a few minutes later. The coach was with them. Adam's stepdad was hopping mad.

"I'll kill him." He was saying. "This is just like him to ruin my day. He's hell bent on making me look stupid in front of all my friends."

They kept quizzing me about where he could be but I didn't know where he was so I couldn't tell them. It was now only forty minutes before kick off. They kept looking at their watches.

The coach said that he would have to go and be with his players. He said that he would have to get one of the substitutes to get changed and stretched off.

Adam's stepdad was getting angrier by the minute. He kept pacing back and forth like a caged tiger. He was winding his watch up and muttering threats under his breath.

"I'll ground him for a month. He won't kick a ball again until he leaves home. I'll never forgive him for making me look such an idiot."

Mr Smith apologised. He said that it was too much to expect such a young boy to be able to accept such a lot of responsibility. He was saying that none of this would have happened if it weren't for him. He said that he had pushed Adam too hard. It was ridiculous. He had been the best person in Adam's life. He had nothing to feel guilty about. He was the one person who had helped Adam realise his dream.

Time passed by and there was still no sign of him. There was now only half an hour to go before the kick off. Everybody was looking at me. As Adam's best friend, they thought that I should know where he was but I had no idea whatsoever.

Adam's stepfather led me to one side. He leant over to be near my ear and whispered, "If it turns out that you knew all along where he was, you'll never set foot in my house again. Do you understand, boy?"

I nodded at him, but said nothing. There was nothing I could say. I didn't know anything.

The coach decided to get one of the substitutes warmed up. Time was running out. Adam's mum started talking about the possibility that he could have been run over or something. She asked us if there was somewhere that the two of us went to when we were upset, or when we wanted to be away from other people. I was a bit hesitant. Of course I was thinking about our den but we had always kept it a secret. His mum said that he would be feeling awful if nerves had got the better of him. He would be thinking about how he had let everybody down. She said that, if they could get to him quickly, there was still time to persuade him to rush to the ground and play.

My head was spinning, full of contradicting ideas. I decided to show her where our den was. Adam's mum drove us there as fast as she could. I had never known her drive so fast. When we got there, the den was empty. There was no sign of him. He hadn't been there at all.

His mum was clearly upset. She quizzed me some more but I couldn't tell her anything. We went back to the ground to see if he had arrived. On the way back Adam's mum gave me her mobile phone so that I could phone Adam's dad to see if he knew anything. I phoned but there was no reply.

When we got back to the ground the players were lining up to be introduced to the Lord Mayor of Birmingham who was the guest of honour.

Adam was still nowhere to be seen. His stepdad was really angry. He kept apologising to his friends. The coach looked up to where we were, but all Adam's mum could do was shrug her shoulders.

The coach got the substitute to take off his tracksuit. He then put his arm around his shoulders and started drilling him with last minute instructions.

Adam's mum called the police to inform them that he was missing. They told her to wait in the car park of the ground and they would meet her there. They said they wanted me to be there as well so that they could ask me some questions. We walked out to the car park to find Adam standing there with his dad. Adam said that he was sorry for any problems he had caused but he also said that he would refuse to play unless his dad could be there to see him.

Adam's mum was a mixture of anger and happiness. She didn't say anything to him, just hugged him close.

There was an official from the club who had been following the whole story. He said Adam's dad could go in for free.

Adam's dad said, "What about him?" he was pointing at Adam's stepdad. His mum told them just to go in and she would sort it out. The problem was that he shouldn't have been there because it wasn't his weekend. They went in and Adam ran down to the manager to make his apologies.

I expected the manager to be really angry but he was all right about it. I couldn't hear what he was saying but he put his hands on the side of Adam's head and ruffled his hair. He sent Adam in to get changed.

By this time, the match was well underway. I went back to Mr Smith and the others from our school. Our team had quite a lot of the game but we were failing to take our chances. The game stayed tied at nil-nil until about five minutes from the end of the first half. The other team made a break away run from just inside their own half. They scored with a blistering shot from way outside the penalty area. Our goalkeeper never had a chance.

I saw Adam's mum come into the ground just before half time. She had waited to explain to the police that Adam had turned up. She hadn't missed much though. Adam hadn't got on the pitch yet and we were losing one-nil.

All the way through the first half, I had looked over at the bench every time the ball went out of play. I was looking to see if Adam was going to be brought on. When the teams came out at half time I looked all around to see where Adam was but it was no use. He hadn't been sent on yet. He took up his place sitting with the other substitutes on the bench.

It was a game that I am sure was harder to watch than to play. I felt involved in every challenge and every tackle. We came close to scoring several times without actually making it. The pressure was almost too much to bear. I spent as much time with my eyes closed as I did with them open. Every time they got near our goal, I closed my eyes and every time we got near their goal, I closed them again!

Adam was sent on after about a quarter of an hour. With only thirty minutes to go it was too much to expect him to make much of an impression. Adam had other ideas though. He charged and chased after every ball. He seemed determined to make up for missing so much of the game by trying four times as hard in the time that he had. He gave away a couple of fouls as he tried so hard to win every fifty-fifty ball. It was as though he was possessed. He was shoulder challenging and throwing his arms around. He was just about the smallest player on the pitch. Many of the other players were six years older than him. None of that bothered him. It was clear that he was going to do every single thing in his power to help his side win the cup.

It was hard to say how much of it was down to Adam, but when others saw him trying so hard and being so determined they all seemed to pick their own game up. There was a renewed vigour about the team.

This new attitude paid off when Adam's team were awarded a penalty. To his credit, I could see Adam volunteer to take it but it had been decided before the match that another player would take it. The penalty was converted and so, with about ten minutes to go, the score was one-all.

There was a surge of attacking football that came from Adam's team. They came forward in waves. Attack after attack brought them nearer and nearer to the goal. I felt certain that one of the attacks must result in a goal. I desperately wanted it to be scored by Adam. All the kids from our school started chanting, "Adam! Adam! Adam!" and we all cheered wildly every time he got the ball.

Their goalkeeper made a big clearance and Adam picked up the ball. We all stood up as he ran towards the defence. He beat player after player and we all jumped up and down as he got closer to the goal. Their centre-half came crashing down and lunged forward to tackle Adam. He went spilling to the ground and the ball bobbled free. One of Adam's teammates pounced upon it and smashed it into the net. It was a goal. With only minutes to go, we were leading two-one.

The opposition got the game started as quickly as they could and began attacking as though their lives depended upon it. It was no use, though. Adam's team hung on for the last few minutes. When the final whistle went, it was two goals to one and Adam's team had won the cup. All of Adam's team hugged each other and shook hands. Adam ran straight over to the side of the pitch and jumped over the side into the stands. He ran straight up to his dad and hugged him. There were tears in his eyes. Adam's stepdad called him over to meet his friends but Adam ran past him and over to where we were standing. He hugged Mr Smith and me at the same time. Mr Smith asked him what he was crying for. Adam said that he didn't know.

Watching Adam go up to receive his medal made me feel really proud. I couldn't have felt more proud if I had won it myself.

Adam's stepdad wanted Adam to go back home for a party but he told him and his mum that he had already agreed to go back to my house. It was a bit of a white lie. We hadn't made any such agreement at all. We went off together though. Later in the evening, we decided to pay a surprise visit to Adam's dad. When we got there, we could see through the windows that he had been doing some celebrating of his own. He was fast asleep in his armchair surrounded by beer cans and an empty bottle of whisky.

Adam didn't mind. He was used to it. We went back to the den for a while and then we went back to my house. Adam was staying the night. We went to bed and my mum made us some cocoa. By the time she bought it up to us, Adam was fast asleep.

It is a sin to
tell yourself
that you
cannot do…
ANYTHING!

## Chapter Five

Adam's dad got into quite a lot of trouble because he wasn't supposed to see Adam on certain weekends. There was no provision in the court order for cup finals. He had to eat a bit of humble pie where Adam's stepdad was concerned. He had to apologise for seeing Adam and he had to assure him that it wouldn't happen again. We knew it broke his heart.

Mr Smith was as solid as ever. He kept on taking us to matches and doing extra training with us. When we left primary school, he continued to work with us. I carried on playing, but Adam left me well behind by the time we had moved to senior school. He was picked to play for district teams and then for the county team. When I wasn't playing, I would go and watch Adam. Mr Smith picked us both up and drove us around the country. The only time that Adam's stepdad showed any interest was when there was some big occasion and he could show off to his friends.

Adam's dad went to see him as often as he could. His knees got progressively worse. He was beginning to find it difficult to get around. He had his crutches with him permanently now and, even with them, he moved very slowly. I know that Adam felt very sorry for him. How different his life would have been if he had fulfilled his promise and gone on to play for Manchester United.

Adam still kept his diary. He wrote down brief details of all the football he played. Every week, he wrote down whether or not he thought he was any nearer to playing for Man.U. Mr Smith pushed Adam as hard as Adam had ever pushed himself. Their training sessions lasted until quite late into the evenings. Adam did a lot of speed and stamina work with his clubs so Mr Smith concentrated on skills training. Adam did some sort of training or playing every night of the week. There was one night that Adam told his mum that he was training until 7.30pm but he really left at 5.30pm. He sneaked off to see his dad at this time.

His dad was living in a fairly tatty flat. I think that Adam and I were the only people who visited him from one week to the next.

When we were round at Adam's dad's flat one night, we found a letter. Adam didn't tell his dad that he had seen it. Seeing it was a major shock to Adam, though. The letter said that Adam's dad could have an operation to halt the decline of his knee injury. The problem was that it would cost £5000. It may as well have been five million pounds. There was no way he could ever afford it. Adam told me that he wished he were ten years older and playing for Man.U. That way he could buy his dad the best treatment in the world.

Adam did have a hard childhood but he also had a wonderful childhood. Other boys were still jealous of him and gave him a hard time. Michael Jones was at the same senior school as us and never missed an opportunity to pick on Adam. The tension between his parents was as intense as ever but this was all completely overshadowed by football. Adam always felt wonderful about his football and, when he was eleven and a half years old, something happened that made him one of the happiest boys alive.

Mr Smith went to Adam's house one night with a very special letter. Adam's face lit up when he heard the news. He had been picked to play for England Schoolboys. It was the best of times. I have never known a boy be so happy.

Adam and I went over to his dad's house. When we told him the news, he pushed his crutches to the ground and hugged Adam. I thought he was going to hug the life out of him. When he eventually put Adam down, he sort of moved his arms around and did a one-legged dance. If Adam was one of the happiest boys in the world, then his dad was definitely the happiest dad in the world.

Adam playing for England was one of the biggest things to happen to our school. The whole school was given the day off to go and watch him play. Our old primary school was also closed for the day. The build up to the big day was wonderful. We got so excited that we couldn't talk about anything else.

There were about eight coaches that went down from our area. We had banners made up. Some had "ENGLAND" written on them and some just said "ADAM". England were playing Scotland and we won 3-1. Adam scored a great goal directly from a free kick. Adam was brimming with happiness. This was just the pick-me-up that Adam's dad needed as well. It seemed that life couldn't get any better. Life could get better, though, and it did. A few weeks later, Adam received a letter that was even better than the one telling him that he had been picked to play for England.

Adam's letter informed him that he had been selected to attend a trial for Aston Villa. Adam was delirious. He couldn't control his excitement. He did an involuntary dance.

Two days later, his excitement was to rise to even greater heights. It seemed that Villa scouts were not the only ones watching the England v. Scotland match. Manchester United had scouts there as well. Now Man.U. also invited him for a trial. He said he felt as though he had looked upon the face of God. His whole life had been a preparation for this moment.

The two offers were quite different. Villa's was a weekend at their training ground. If he were successful, he would play for their under 15's team. That was the team that was one below the youth team. He would be able to stay at home and stay at our school. He would just have to train after school and play at weekends. He would be on their books, though, and that's the important thing. He would be one step nearer to his dream of being a professional footballer. Of course, Adam would, by far, prefer to play for Manchester United, but he was aware that only a very few people get to play for them, so he would be satisfied if he didn't quite make that but he did get to play for Villa.

Manchester United's trial was a much bigger deal. He had to stay in Manchester for a week. He was to stay with a local family. He was to train and play every day. They looked at his attitude and fitness as well as his skills. If he were successful, then he would be signed on to play for their under 15's. The difference was that Manchester United were also offering a place in their School of Excellence. Adam, if he were successful, would have to live near Manchester and attend a school that was centred on football. He would train in the mornings, do school work in the afternoons and train again in the evenings.

Being successful at the Man.U. trials would solve all of Adam's problems and make his life perfect in an instant. We talked long and hard about the difference it would make to our lives. It would be difficult for us to be apart because we had spent almost every day together since we could remember.

The trials loomed large in both our lives. The Villa weekend came first. Adam was completely pumped up for it. His mum kept going on about him not eating. She kept saying that he would collapse if he didn't eat properly. I knew what it was like for him though. During the week leading up to the trial, I could hardly eat myself. I couldn't get to see him play because the trials were all carried out behind closed doors. Upon his return, I could tell that he had done really well. He wasn't showing off, but he was confident that he had done his best. All he could do now was to keep his fingers crossed and wait for the letter to come through the door. In the meantime he had the little matter of the Man.U. trials to deal with.

Preparing for the Villa trials had been a very tense time but as the days went by whilst we waited for the Manchester United trials, neither of us could eat nor sleep properly. We could barely breathe properly. I helped him pack and travelled up to Manchester with him. His mum took us up. Mr Smith came to the station to see us off. I watched everybody going about their normal business. They had no idea that this was no normal day.

Waiting at home was really hard. Adam phoned me every night, but it was still an awful wait and seemed to last for ever. In his nightly phone calls, he did say that he was very pleased with the way things were going. The coaches kept telling them all not to run themselves into the ground but to pace themselves. It was the same for everybody though. Each and every boy was desperate to impress so they gave one hundred percent in every session. Adam said that there were some great players there but he wasn't going to let any of them overshadow him.

The trial came and went but the tension remained. It was a bit like waiting for an exam result. Adam waited for the postman each day and I waited for his phone call. The wait was particularly agonising because there was no deadline. All the clubs said was that they would send out the letters as soon as the decisions had been made.

Adam at last received a letter. It was from Aston Villa. It was great news. They wanted him to sign for them. Adam was delighted. He could relax now in the certain knowledge that he would definitely be signing for a Premiership club. All he had to do was to sit tight and wait to find out if Man.U. were also going to offer him a place.

The days seemed to take weeks to pass. After what seemed like an age, Adam received another letter. It was just like the one before, but this time it was addressed to his stepdad. As no one else was about, Adam opened it. It wasn't from Manchester United, though. It was another one from

Aston Villa. It was a secret, unofficial one. In it they offered Adam's stepdad a cash incentive to get Adam's signature. This wasn't exactly illegal but it was against the FA rules. No payments were supposed to be made to underage players or their parents. The amount that they were offering was absolutely massive. The sum that was written in the letter was £6000. Adam hid the letter so that his stepfather wouldn't get to read it. He knew that the lure of £6000 would mean more to him than Adam's dream of playing for Manchester United. He knew that his stepdad would try to make him sign for Villa if it meant that he could get his hands on all that money.

I was the only person that Adam told about the letter and the money. We just kept the offer to ourselves whilst we waited for Man.U. to write.

It was a long time before we got the news from Man.U. but when it came it wasn't the news that we were hoping for. They weren't offering him a place. I was heartbroken. I felt somehow certain that they were going to offer him a place. They'd seen him play out of his skin for England. Even by his own very high standards, he said that he had played at his very best during the trial week. I think that I was more upset than Adam. He said that he was disappointed but that he was still going to sign for a big Premiership club.

Adam had always impressed me, not only as a footballer, but also as a person. His ability to take this setback so well impressed me more than anything.

That was until I found out the truth.

Adam let me read his diary. In fact he often asked me to check it to make sure that he hadn't missed anything out. As I flicked through it, I found that he had been offered a place at Manchester United but had turned it down in favour of a place at Aston Villa.

I just couldn't believe he would do such a thing. Everybody knew that his heart's desire was to play for Manchester United. When I confronted him about it, he was reluctant to talk. I demanded an explanation. I just wanted to know why he would do such a thing.

Adam told me that the reason he turned down Manchester was because he didn't want to live away from home. I found that hard to believe. I read through his diary some more and the truth was revealed. Adam had written back to Aston Villa and pretended to be his stepdad. He told them to leave an envelope with all the money in Adam's kit bag. Adam then put the money through his dad's door with a note saying it was from an anonymous well-wisher so that he could pay for his knee operation.

Adam had given up the most important thing in his life for his father and he wasn't going to tell anyone – not even me.

I had always liked Adam. I had always respected him. Now I admired him in a way that words could scarcely express.

Anything that you want to do – you can do.

## Chapter Six

This was a defining moment in Adam's life. No longer was he Adam, the good footballer. He was now Adam, the lad who was on Villa's books. Adam became a lot happier and a lot more confident. We spent as much of our free time together as we ever did. The time that we had free together was diminishing, though. Adam had to spend a lot of time training and my workload was getting heavier at school. By this time I had decided on aiming for a university education. We met up to chat most evenings. We listened to music and just treated each other as a sounding board.

Adam continued to keep his diary. He still had the dream of playing for Man.U. but his diary entries were now all about playing for Villa. Adam had carried out some research into the club's history. There had been quite a high number of sixteen year olds that had made their first team debuts and there had been lots of seventeen year olds who had played for the first team. As far as Adam was concerned, his debut couldn't come a day too soon.

As time passed by, Adam and I spent more time at his dad's house. All that stuff about when and where Adam could meet with his dad had dropped along the wayside. Adam just called on his dad whenever he felt like it. Adam's dad was still in a bad way. Although he had had his operation, he was still a bitter man. All the operation had done was to halt his decline. He still had very limited mobility. He was a man who had the joys of the world dangled in front of him and then had them taken away in the cruellest of ways.

Adam's dad desperately wanted his son to be a professional footballer, that was very plainly obvious. I felt that there was an intensely cruel irony in the situation though. Every day he saw in his son a constant reminder of all that he himself had been promised. It was as though fate were saying to him, "Do you remember every minute of pain that your injury inflicted upon you? Do you remember all of the hope that was dashed in an instant?" Despite all of this evident and thinly disguised emotion, Adam's dad clearly harboured as much hope for his son's future as ever Adam held for himself.

Adam's dad always made an effort when we went to visit when we were younger. As we grew up, though, he bothered less and less. He made less effort to hide his beer cans and whisky bottles. His journeys beyond his front door became increasingly rare. The amount of fresh air that he let into his flat also diminished. We still liked going round there. I look back and think of it as fairly sad now but, in all honesty, I don't think that we talked about it much at the time. It wasn't really an issue. That was just the way it was.

Adam's mum was always an attentive mother but she seemed to me to be a little indifferent to his career. I think that much of this was because of his father's injury. She took quite a few opportunities to talk to Adam about it. Sometimes she talked about it when there was just Adam there but on more than one occasion she talked about it when I was there as well. She talked of how his dad had been such a happy teenager. She said that he was always happy and laughing. His was clearly a great footballing talent. Adam's gran had kept a scrapbook. He had clearly made as many headlines as Adam had by the time of his injury. Adam's mum kept telling him that he might not make it as a footballer and that he should work hard at school to get his qualifications in case his footballing career didn't work out well. I don't think that she was deliberately trying to demoralise Adam. I think that she just wanted to make sure that if anything ever happened to him, such as an injury, that it wouldn't be the end of his world. Like most teenagers, we thought that the chance of such an occurrence was a million to one. It never crossed our minds that we would be anything but a hundred percent fit and well. Even the evidence that we saw in his dad's case didn't influence us.

The words that his mother spoke were to prove more prophetic than she could ever have anticipated. Adam and I were constantly having run-ins with Michael Jones. His dislike for Adam had grown into a fair degree of hate. Adam was a lot more confident as a teenager than he had ever been as a child. There had been several scuffles between the two, but Michael knew that I would never be too far away. Whenever a disagreement came to a bit of a punch up, I would always step in and take Adam's side. I was over six feet tall by the time I was fourteen and I could sort the likes of Michael Jones out without too much trouble. I gave him a bloody nose on more than one occasion.

Michael was showing off his footballing skills in front of some girls and keeping the ball in the air. He was quite good at it and he could do some pretty good tricks. Then Adam came along and the girls asked him to do it as well. Of course, Adam was much better at it than Michael and the girls started applauding him and giggling and cheering. Adam thought nothing about this at the time and just gave the ball back to Michael and carried on about his business. Michael took it to heart though. He thought that Adam had deliberately shown him up in front of the girls and so he waited for him after school. Adam used to walk across some wasteland to go and get his bus to the Villa training ground. Michael lay in wait for him.

It wasn't much of a fight. Michael ambushed him. He jumped out on him from behind and knocked him to the ground. In the course of the beating that he took, Adam sustained an injury. It was one of the worst kind of injuries that a footballer could suffer. He damaged the ligaments in his knee.

When we found out, we all feared the worst. I know we all feared that history could be repeating itself. Adam's mum was distraught. I think it hit her harder than anyone. Adam was taken to the Accident and Emergency department at the local hospital. He was asking for me, so his mum called me. I called Mr Smith. Adam's dad and his stepdad were there as well. They kept asking me what had happened, but it was just like cup final day. I couldn't tell them anything because I didn't know anything. I wasn't there.

Adam was taken into theatre and was operated on immediately. It was an agonising wait for all those who were close to him. It wasn't just his present that we were worried about; it was his future. We all knew that this could spell the end of his footballing dreams. All of the pain that his dad went through so many years ago was coming back to haunt him. We didn't say much to each other; we all knew exactly what the others were thinking. Mr Smith had the presence of mind to phone Villa to tell them what had happened. The club sent their own doctor over to assess him. He arrived in a very short time indeed. This sent us into something of a panic because we felt that it was obvious that the club thought that it was a serious matter.

The doctor was clearly known to the hospital because they waved him through with a degree of VIP treatment. We could see them talking through a window. They were all shaking their heads. We could all sense that the news was far from good. The Villa doctor was handed an X-ray and when he put it up to the light we could all see that his face contorted. Adam's dad said, "Oh, God. No!" and Mr Smith put his arm around him. Adam's mum started crying.

The police arrived and started asking us loads of questions. They asked me the most, of course. They seemed convinced that I knew something about it. The fight had been reported to the police and they had already taken Michael Jones down to the station. From the questions that they asked, it was obvious that they had been told that Adam had arranged to meet Michael there to settle their differences. I knew this wasn't true. If Adam had been walking into a fight, he would have made sure that I was with him.

One of the doctors came out and told us that it would be some time before they could tell us any news. Adam's mum started crying more than ever. She had been as brave as she could be for as long as she could be. Adam's stepdad tried to comfort her but she pushed him away and went out and sat on a chair by herself. She said that she was going to take Michael to court. Adam's dad was saying that he would sort Michael out himself. It was an angry and anxious time.

After a while, the Villa doctor came out and spoke to us. He told us that it was too early to say how serious it would be in the long term, but in the short term, he hoped that Adam would make a full recovery. This didn't help much at all. The immediate relief was, in many ways, less important. We wanted to know if Adam still had a future as a professional footballer. All that the doctors would tell us was that Adam had been a very lucky young man. He said that if the damage had been done a centimetre or two the other way, he may not have played sport at any level ever again. He didn't realise how important this was to us. The injury was so poignant to all of us because his father had ended his career with a knee injury. Now we wanted to know whether or not Adam's hopes were still alive. The doctor wouldn't be drawn, but he said that modern surgery was such that Adam would be able to do some light training in a few weeks. He said that if early tests showed that Adam could run without any pain, then the future would look bright and there would be no reason why he shouldn't go on and become a professional footballer. He was honest, though. He told us that if Adam did show early signs of pain, then we should take this as a sign that his knee may not be able to take the punishing rigours of the life of a pro-footballer.

I waited until late in the evening before I could go in and see him. His face was a lot more swollen and bruised than I had expected it to be. It seemed that Michael had really lost it. All of the years of frustration had clearly shaken his emotions up to boiling point. Adam found it difficult to talk. He said that he was no nearer to playing for Man.U. I told him that he was no further away either. I said the words to try and reassure him but I wasn't sure that they were true. But, oh, how I prayed they would be!

Mr Smith drove me home. He seemed a lot more at ease than anybody else. He said that he saw in Adam a person who had enormous inner strength. He reminded me how Adam and I had faced adversity out at sea but we dug deep into our reserves of character, and deep inner strength had seen us through. He told me that he had faith in Adam.

Adam's dad didn't take this period of time very well at all. It seemed to act like a magnifying glass to his state of mind. He became more bitter, more resentful and altogether angrier. I went round to see him several times. I usually had the feeling that he was really pleased to see me, but at the same time I felt as though I was in the way. I had the feeling that he resented me. He resented my ability to walk around freely whilst he and his son couldn't and he resented me intruding on his grief, remorse and pity.

Adam perked up remarkably quickly. He sat up in bed and talked and joked with visitors. His conversation centred around how long he would be out of action and how many games he would miss. It didn't seem to occur to him that his dreams were being threatened.

After eight days, he started physiotherapy. It was all very slow progress at first. He underwent a few minutes' work each day and he gradually moved his legs up and down a little more each time.

Adam told his mum that he didn't want Michael prosecuted. He said that he just felt sorry for him. His mum was happy to leave it at that. There was nothing to be gained by pressing charges. Everybody at school knew what he had done. He became something of an outcast and Adam's popularity grew from that time on.

After about five weeks, Adam started walking about quite freely without support. That in itself was something of a relief. At least the injury was nowhere as serious as his dad's. Adam called round to my house and told me that he wanted to watch me playing "Hit the Sign". It was the game that we'd always played together as children. It was easy to play individually. Adam sat on a wall and watched. It was a bit like old times. After a while, Adam confessed that he had asked me to come out for a special reason. It was time for him to try out his knee. The physio had told him to try jogging on it when he felt it was ready. He wanted me to be there because he didn't want to be alone if it was bad news.

Of course, I asked him if he was sure it wasn't too soon. He assured me that it wasn't because he had been told exactly what to expect. If there was some general soreness around the knee, this was nothing to worry about. In fact, it was only to be expected. There was a specific part of the knee that he had to concentrate on and, if it didn't give way, then everything would be fine.

Adam stood by the side of the grass and took some deep breaths. He gave me a last look and then he went for it. He jogged slowly several paces onto the grass. A small smile came onto his face and he raised his eyebrows. So far, so good. Then he jogged a little further. He turned around with a big smile on his face. It was good news. The knee was standing up really well. He lifted his knee up a little further and he ran a little faster. He stood and stared at me with his hands on his hips. It was a wonderful relief. I ran over and threw my arms around him. It felt just great!

It was great news. Adam was back playing football eleven weeks after the injury. Mr Smith had been right. Adam had a sack load of inner strength and character.

A teacher's
influence will
last
forever.

## Chapter Seven

Adam and I both worked hard during our final years at school. He did OK in his GCSEs but, as ever, there was only one career that he had on his mind. I got all the exams I needed and went to University to do a degree in English and Journalism.

Adam became more popular as we got older. There was a growing entourage of young admirers, as he got closer to playing for the first team. When he was told that he would be on the bench for the first time, there was no happier admirer than me. It happened to fall on the same day that I had an important exam. There must be some sort of rule that makes it certain in my life that really important things happen to fall on the same day.

We arranged for me to go up on the train. It was a very close call. I had to get a taxi to wait for me so that I could dash straight to the train station. Adam and I had arranged it all down to the last minute. He wanted to meet me off the train and take me to the ground himself. His parents were going to be there, but he said that he wanted me there as a sort of good luck mascot. I breezed through the exam. My mind was flying. It was one of those days that I felt more alive than any normal day. My best mate was going to make his first team debut in the Premiership. I felt like an ordinary person being swept away into a new, glamorous world. Premiership football. It was like a dream.

There are times when I feel that my mind is particularly sharp. Every word that I want to use is ready and waiting for me. Nothing is laboured and I feel really great. That day was the first time that I felt that way. My mate was actually going to play in the Premiership. I felt like royalty. Villa were playing Chelsea. It was such a thrill to think that Adam was good enough to be competing against the best in England or even the best in the world. The Chelsea central defender had a World Cup winner's medal so really you could say that he was competing with the best in the world. To think that I would be meeting all of the players after the match! I felt I had swapped my life for somebody more fortunate than myself.

I skipped out of the college and bounced down the steps to the waiting taxi. When people talk about having a spring in their step when they are feeling good, I know exactly what they mean. I remember having boundless energy that day. My mate, my best mate, was going to be playing for Villa against Chelsea. I had tickets next to Mr Smith and Adam's dad. I was going to go out with Adam after the match to celebrate. I had bought a Villa scarf, of course, so had Adam's dad and Mr Smith. Oh, how I hoped and prayed that he would be the star of the match. If hard work and determination meant anything, then he deserved to be. He had faced imminent death at sea and found the strength and courage to come through. He had faced serious injury and held his faith. He deserved it. If anybody deserved it, he did. I was as excited as a child on Christmas day.

I got to the station on time and tipped the taxi driver. That may not seem like the most important detail to remember but, for someone living on a student's loan, it was a very big deal. I never planned to do it. I just got carried away with the excitement of it all.

When I walked into the station, there was an announcement that said that the Birmingham train had been cancelled. I couldn't believe it. It was like there was too much air in my lungs. I checked with a railway worker, but he just confirmed that the train had been cancelled. My reaction was all out of proportion. I felt like someone had died. The prospect of missing Adam's debut was unthinkable.

The train company had laid on a coach but, as it was going to all of the stations that the train would have stopped at, it would have meant missing the match. It was unthinkable. I couldn't make myself face up to the prospect of missing it. I kept telling them that my friend was to make his debut against Chelsea but I knew that wouldn't make the situation any better. They made some phone calls to their head office but nobody seemed able to magic up a solution.

I phoned Adam with the bad news and I could tell that the news knocked him sideways as well. This was not what he wanted on his big day. When you're making your debut for Aston Villa against Chelsea, you need everything to run smoothly. He suggested that I see if I could get a connecting train from one of the stations to Birmingham so that I might be able to make it on time.

I asked people at the station to look into it, which, to their credit, they did. They tried everything to find a way for me to make it on time but it just wasn't going to happen. It was hopeless. I rang Adam back and explained the situation but he had been doing some thinking. He told me to get a taxi all of the way and that he would pay for it. At first I said that was ridiculous. It would cost him hundreds of pounds but then I remembered how much he earned and I agreed. It was so decadent. It was the height of luxury.

I phoned around a few taxi companies and asked them if they could get me to Villa Park for seven thirty but they had worse news for me. Because it was rush hour time, there was no way that any of them could get me there on time.

I was reluctant to do it but there was nothing else for it. I phoned Adam and told him the bad news. I wouldn't be able to get there until sometime after kick off, that's if I got there to watch any of the match at all. I could tell that it was far from what Adam wanted for his big day, but, as there was absolutely nothing that we could do about it, we just had to accept it.

I got into a taxi and sat back. There was nothing I could do but try and make myself accept the situation and make myself calm down.

Then the day took another twist when Adam gave me another call on my mobile. He sounded really happy on the other end of the phone. He had mentioned to the club's chairman what had happened and, in an amazing gesture of spontaneous generosity, he said that he would send his personal helicopter for me. He was already sending it for someone else who was in the south of England so he said that he would send it for me as well. It really was the most amazing change of fortune. The taxi driver took me to the place where we had been told to go and within half an hour I was sitting in a helicopter on my way to Villa Park. I had never been in a plane or helicopter before. It was an exciting time. When I say that I was on my way to Villa Park, I really mean that I was on my way to Villa Park. The helicopter put us down in the middle of the pitch. It was a strange feeling being in a football ground that was empty. The gates hadn't opened yet and there I was walking across one of the most famous pieces of turf in the world and there was Adam waiting for me.

Adam couldn't stay with me for very long because he had to go and start warming up. Something I found out from Adam was that professional footballers do a two-hour warm up before any match. I was taken to the executive suite and given tea and sandwiches. It felt as though I had walked into another world.

As the crowd began to come into the ground, I went over to meet up with Adam's dad and Mr Smith. They couldn't believe the day that I had lived through. We laughed and joked our way though the build up. My mind swirled with the sounds of the crowd and the music coming over the PA system.

When the teams walked out, it was hard to know which of us was the proudest. Adam ran out in his tracksuit and juggled the ball out on to the pitch. I knew that I was biased, but it seemed to me that Adam was the most skilful player on the pitch. In my eyes, he stood out as a genius, and that was just during the warm up! I could tell by the beaming smiles on their faces that Mr Smith and Adam's dad were every bit as proud of him as I was.

The boss had told him that he was going to get a run out but he didn't know when. The game was a turgid affair. Villa went into the lead but Chelsea got a goal back. Half time came and there was no sign of Adam coming on but we hoped that he would come out in the starting eleven for the second half.

When the teams came out we craned to see if Adam's slight frame was among them. It was no use. He trailed out with the other substitutes still decked out in his tracksuit.

The second half continued with Villa grinding out a slightly better performance. They scored after about twenty minutes and then packed the defence to hold onto their lead. As each minute passed, we all looked at our watches continuously, waiting for Adam to announce himself on the big stage at last. But time passed and the final whistle was blown. Adam's big day had come and gone and we were all left in a monumental anticlimax.

Mr Smith helped Adam's dad home at the end of the match. They told me to tell Adam to keep his chin up and to have some patience. They said that his big day would come soon enough and, of course, I agreed with them.

Adam and I went for a walk after the match. He was surprisingly philosophical. He knew that his time would come. He seemed really calm. It was as though he was almost relieved not to have been sent on.

As part of my work in journalism, some years later I found out that this manager did the same to all his young players. He believed that they would get rid of all of their nerves on their dummy run.

It was a day of wildly contrasting emotions for me. The high times and the low times of Adam's life were always the high times and low times in my life. That day left me spinning.

Adam did make his debut later in that season. It was in a cup match abroad. He came on as a substitute and scored. Adam stepped up into premiership football with the same consummate ease that he had whenever he stepped up a level. Adam ironically made his home debut against Chelsea in the cup. He was in the starting eleven this time and scored in that match as well. I made an altogether less eventful journey to that match and watched it with Mr Smith and Adam's dad.

Adam and I went out to a nightclub that night. We went to a couple more on other occasions. We were never really clubbers, though. It was not our scene.

When I completed my degree, Adam came to watch me collect my cap and gown. We went to a nightclub on that night as well.

On Adam's wall he had two pictures. One was of him playing for England schoolboys and the other one was of Adam standing next to me wearing my cap and gown.

If you tell yourself you can or if you tell yourself you can't – you are telling the truth.

## Chapter Eight

There were lots of big matches in those early days. The fans took to Adam. They chanted his name and sang songs about him. He set the Premiership alive. He won lots of awards like "Man of the Match" or "Player of the Year". He never got the Premiership's top scorer record in those early days but he was always there or thereabouts. The press loved him and the public loved him too.

I continued to go and watch him as often as I could. We went on some fabulous holidays. Adam was never foolish with his new found wealth, but he did enjoy spending his money. He bought some really nice houses in some really nice parts of the world. He was pleased to invite me to be his houseguest and I was pleased to accept. We had various girlfriends and they came along with us.

My career was coming along nicely. I was fortunate enough to work for some quality papers and periodicals. Adam had another milestone in his life. He was selected to play for the England Under 21 squad. He was very proud of his inclusion in the team and he played his heart out. He rang me after his under 21's debut. I was working in the Far East at the time. He was bubbling with excitement. He told me that there were very few things that would make him feel better than he felt that night. He said that winning the FA cup or the League title would top it – and, of course, playing for Man.U. would make him happier than anything else.

Life was good. Our lives were taking us to different places but our friendship was as warm and close as ever. I know that it gave Adam a lot of pleasure to be able to buy his mum a new house in the country. It inspired me to write an article about how money changes people. I came to the conclusion that it's a bit like becoming a celebrity. It makes nice people nicer still and it makes nasty people nastier still. It definitely made Adam an even bigger Mr Nice Guy. He always had time for fans and members of the public. He would stand and sign autographs, sometimes literally for hours, and he was never too busy to stop and have his picture taken with members of the public.

They say that the best way to make God laugh is to tell him your five-year plan. When Adam's life was nothing but a joyous celebration something happened that was to set him back more than his knee injury. It wasn't a physical setback but mentally it was a cruel blow. We had known for some time that his dad's injury was part of a bigger health problem. His dad was certainly suffering but we had no way of knowing just how serious it was. It was very serious though. The doctors told him that he was getting worse. We could see that with each passing year his mobility deteriorated and his hands shook a lot as well, but now we were being told that, if they couldn't find a cure for him, then he would end up permanently confined to a wheelchair.

Adam had already proved his love for his father by giving up his coveted place with Man.U. Schoolboys. Now, he made a vow that, if there were a hospital on earth that could help him, he would find it and help his dad to get better.

Adam had already spent a lot of money on his father. He bought him a ground floor flat. There was a person on call that could help if he ever needed anything. There were also people who came in to clean and tidy for him. Now Adam was prepared to spend every penny he had if it meant that he could help his father get better.

Adam sent his dad to America for a series of operations. He paid for a nurse to travel with him and look after him. Adam never talked about money but I got the impression that it was costing him every penny he had, if not more. I went with Adam to see his dad off at the airport. It was quite a tearful event. To see somebody who has harboured dreams of playing for Manchester United reduced to hobbling around on crutches was a sad affair indeed. The idea that one day he could be confined to a wheelchair was a dreadful concept.

We had been told, in no uncertain terms, that the procedures that they were embarking upon were far from risk free. If he didn't have the procedures, he could end up permanently in a wheelchair but if he did have the procedure, and it was unsuccessful, he would still end up in a wheelchair but it would happen much sooner. If the operation were successful, his mobility would be dramatically improved. The big problem was that there was only a twenty five percent chance of success. It was one hell of a big gamble.

There's an old cliché that says that life is full of ups and downs. This was certainly true of Adam's life. Adam was chosen to play for England. It was a massive, huge, enormous thrill not only for Adam but also for us all. England were playing Brazil in a friendly. There was no greater challenge on earth as far as we were concerned. To be playing the greatest footballing nation in the world was a monumental thrill. We had grown to be quite blasé about big occasions but this was a wonderful time for us all.

We all went down to the match together, Adam's mum and stepdad, Mr Smith and me. We knew that Adam had been selected to see if he was mature enough to step into the nation's side for the next World Cup. I spoke to Adam on the afternoon of the match. It was only three or four hours before the kick off yet he was laughing and joking as though he didn't have a care in the world. He said that he just needed to keep focused on the football rather than the occasion and he would be fine. He said that he felt the same kind of feelings when he went out to play for our primary school team all those years ago. He said that he just enjoyed playing football.

I think that we were privileged people. We were earning our living by doing things that we loved; Adam playing football and me writing.

England lost the game but Adam impressed greatly. The England manager singled him out for praise and the press were very generous to him. His England debut had been a great success. We had a big party in a hotel later that evening. It was a great occasion. There was one absentee, though, whose presence would have been greatly appreciated by Adam. He was far away on the other side of the Atlantic. We spoke to him regularly enough but we had no news to speak of. There was no news he could give us. He wouldn't know himself whether the treatment would be a success or not until it had run its course.

Despite the absence of his father, the party was a success. Adam was full of life. We had fine food and wine. This was something that I had become quite used to. As I wasn't training for several hours like Adam, my waistline made a note of any excesses and set upon a course of expansion. I didn't care though. I ate and drank and sang and danced like the rest of those present.

It was around this time that I noticed Adam was getting along a lot better with his stepfather. His stepfather had no control over him now so there was no tension between them. In fact, I would say it was about this time that a shift of power happened in their relationship. There wasn't any great flash of lightning that heralded the moment, but gradually Adam's stepfather started showing him marked respect. When Adam walked into the room his stepdad kind of gave a little nod of his head to acknowledge him. It reminded me of a little bow.

These were happy days but tense days too. I prayed that the operations would be successful. Adam professed not to be religious but he admitted to me that he had been moved to pray himself.

The road to
success
starts with
your next
step.

## Chapter Nine

Playing for England changed Adam's life. He was popular before then but now his celebrity status had been lifted to new heights. It was no longer just football fans that recognised him. It was everybody. Everybody from young children to grannies and granddads recognised him and stopped him wherever he was. They asked him for his autograph and talked to him as though they had known him all their lives.

Adam's picture was a regular feature on the back pages of all the newspapers. The sports journalists had made up their minds that he was the player who would lead England into the next World Cup. Adam gave interviews after matches but he never became one of those players who courted publicity. He was not a shy man. It was just that he preferred to keep some parts of his life private.

For my part, I can look back on that period with a good deal of satisfaction. I was appointed to a new position. It wasn't anywhere near Adam's success, but it was a position that I had aimed towards for some time. It meant that my name and face were recognised by the public. It meant, too, that I had a good salary. This helped because I was able to afford to jet off to foreign parts to watch Adam whenever he played for England. My travels took me to Russia and the Far East and a whole host of places in between. Sometimes Adam was able to invite Mr Smith along. Our relationship was interesting because, although we treated each other as adults, we never stopped calling him Mr Smith. We couldn't bring ourselves to call him by his first name. It was a respect thing.

Adam and I rang America regularly to see how his dad was getting along. It wasn't the best news though. He had an operation and it wasn't the success that they had hoped for. He couldn't walk after it but that wasn't their hope. The purpose of the operation was to try and make him strong enough to have some extended treatment. It meant that the odds of his treatment being successful were now a little worse. I had the feeling that Adam's dad would be able to cope with life in a wheelchair. He had been unable to get around very well for some time. In a sense, it was an extension of his misfortune rather than a complete new catastrophe.

Adam's dad was still angry with the world. He was an angry man, or rather, he was unhappy about his inability to get around. I got the feeling that he was a lot more at ease now that Adam was doing so well. He was a proud man again. I think this did more for him than Adam ever realised because it gave him back all of his natural pride. There was more of a sparkle in his eye than I could ever remember.

Whilst he was undergoing his treatment, I had an opportunity to go and visit him. Adam couldn't get away because he was playing football every week and very often he would play two matches in one week. It was a strange situation. His dad was looking at the most devastating of problems that a man could face and yet he gave out all of the signals that you would expect from a man who felt that life was full of promise. I wondered if he really understood the gravity of his situation. I know Adam did. He told me that he was haunted by visions of his dad in a wheelchair.

The odds that Adam's dad had been given were small. The way that his dad was acting, I began to seriously wonder if he had faced up to it. I could accept that having a son who played for England would make any father feel good about the world but I'm not sure if that would be enough to outweigh the prospect of spending the rest of your life in a wheelchair.

The hospital that he was in was more like a five star hotel. It was a far cry from the flat that we used to go and visit when we were young. He had a buzzer by the side of his bed and with it he could order virtually anything. I had brought some videos with me and we sat and watched Adam play for Villa and England. The shaking in his hands seemed to me to have worsened. He was in relatively good spirits but I was doing my share of worrying and enough for him as well.

I spent several hours with him on most days. During this time I got to talk with the doctors. It seemed that Adam's dad had been keeping some things from us. Part of his procedure was to have an operation on his brain. Adam and I certainly never knew that and his dad was happy in neglecting to tell us about it.

I've come to realise that some things are not spoken of and that some things have no name. As time passed, I came to think that he did realise the odds were stacked heavily against him ever being able to walk again. The reason that he was in such good spirits was that he now had some hope at last.

I was in a difficult position because I had information that Adam would want to know but it was clear that his dad didn't want him to find out how hard things were for him. I received a phone call that put my dilemma on the back burner.

There was a set of very clear rules that governed how transfers were carried out in professional football and the news that Adam rang me with definitely didn't fall within the rules. A secret approach had been made to him from Manchester United. I just knew that he was jumping up and down at the other end of the phone. It was the single most important phone call of my life and it wasn't even happening to me! I could only imagine how excited Adam was. For any player to be approached by a club the size and stature of Manchester United must be a wonderful feeling, but for someone who had harboured ambitions to play for them since childhood, it was a life defining moment.

If, or when, I decided that the time was right to tell Adam how serious his father's treatment was, then I wouldn't shrink from telling him, but now definitely wasn't the right time. Adam put me in an even worse position. I was desperately keen to tell his dad the news but Adam swore me to secrecy. Adam didn't trust his dad not to go telling everyone and he was right. There was no way that Adam's dad could keep that kind of information to himself. No matter how hard he tried, he would just have been compelled to tell every single person that he met. He would have opened the hospital windows and shouted the news to passers by down on the street.

By the time I had arrived home a couple of weeks later, the news was out. Every sporting headline had some mention of Adam and his link with Man.U. Many of the financial pages had news of his transfer as well. The figures involved were astronomical. His dad never did find out that I had known whilst I was out with him. It was a good job because I don't think he would ever have forgiven me.

There were many more headlines over the next few weeks but the transfer did eventually go through. I was at the ground when Adam signed his contract. Although I wasn't a sports correspondent, I used my press credentials to get into the ground. I can honestly say that I have never seen anyone look happier. I had witnessed many of those signing on ceremonies where the new player was paraded carrying his new shirt in front of him. On the surface this was no different, but the pure unadulterated joy on Adam's face was evident for everybody to see. He wasn't jumping around or making any fuss. He just looked like the very happy young man that he was. When all of the other press people had gone, Adam and I had our photograph taken with us holding his new shirt between us. I keep that picture next to my computer to this day.

Mr Smith got in touch with Adam straight away. He never missed an opportunity to congratulate his protégé. Adam had visited our school several times in the early days after he signed for Villa but, as he became a regular first teamer, his time was very precious. Mr Smith asked Adam to do something for him. It was the first time that he had ever asked anything of Adam and Adam jumped at the opportunity to help him out.

Our old school had been given some lottery money. They had built a really big sports complex. It wasn't just for the children of the school; it was for all members of the community. Mr Smith asked Adam if he would come and officially open the centre. It was something of a coup for the school. Not only was Adam a famous "old boy" but at that time he was definitely the hottest property in sport.

Adam's popularity in our hometown knew no bounds. He was afforded respect like royalty wherever he went. This was a very big deal in our hometown and so I decided to seize the moment.

I decided to lay on a surprise for Adam. I contacted every member of our old primary school class and asked them if they would come to the opening and help me give Adam a surprise. The response was overwhelming.

Not only were they all prepared to attend, they were determined to attend. When I embarked upon the mission, I didn't expect to be able to contact all of the class but each person I contacted was only too delighted to put the effort in to contact others. Finding out what everybody was doing with their lives was great fun. Some were mathematicians and some were carpenters. All manner of differing paths had been taken and we all knew how each other had started. We had people who agreed to travel the length and breadth of Britain and we even had people who were willing to make the journey from their new homes in foreign lands. I knew that the day itself would be a great success because the planning of it had been such fun.

The plan for the day was for Adam to cut the ribbon on the door of the complex and to say a few words for the press. Then he was due to come over to the main building of the school and say a few words to the children in an assembly. My plan was to have all of his old pals waiting on the stage to greet him.

The day of the opening caused more of a stir than any of us could have planned for. So many people turned out that it took well over an hour to get Adam up to the door of the complex. The streets all around the school were effectively blocked because so many people had turned out to try and catch a glimpse of their hero.

I crossed my fingers and hoped that the surprise I had in store for him would give him as much pleasure. Adam and his entourage carried out the opening ceremony and fought their way across to the main building of the school.

Mr Smith greeted Adam and took him through the back door and led him to the entrance of the stage. As he walked up the steps and realised that all of his old school pals were there, his eyes lit up. He was clearly taken aback. He went up to every single one of them and shook them by the hand. I thought that Adam's capacity for surprising me had been reached, but surprise me he did. He remembered the name of every single member of our old class.

Every single member of our old class had made it to the reunion and that included Michael Jones. I couldn't understand how he had the nerve to do it after the way he had treated Adam. His actions towards Adam had threatened his entire career. I had certainly not forgotten and I know that Adam would remember every detail.

Adam had all of the power now. He could do anything that he wanted to do. He could demand that Michael leave the building and he would have had to do just that. Michael walked slowly and awkwardly towards Adam. He wasn't at all sure how Adam was going to react. He quietly whispered in Adam's ear that he was glad to finally have the chance to apologise for his actions all of those years ago. He told Adam that he was sorry for being jealous of him. Adam told him that it must have been hard for him. He told him not to worry but to put it behind him. I thought that it was a wonderfully magnanimous gesture. He looked a bit like an archbishop dispensing confession.

Whilst this was going on, all of the children were shouting and screaming and stamping their feet. Adam waved to them and directed them back to their seats with a gesture. Then Adam gave one of the best and most moving speeches that I have ever witnessed.

He spoke about his diary. He told the children that they should never be ashamed of aiming for anything that they wanted in life. He told them that dreams could come true. Then he said, "Look at me!" And everybody cheered. He said some very kind words about me. He told them that I had saved his life at sea when we were children. The truth was far from that but it was very nice of him to say it all the same. He told them that he had been very lucky throughout his life. He told them that his father was very ill in a hospital in America and he asked them all to say a prayer for his recovery. Then he spoke at length about Mr Smith. He told them that Mr Smith was the one person who had helped him to take his first steps towards becoming a professional footballer. He told them that without Mr Smith's training, coaching and advice he may never have realised his dream of playing for Manchester United. He called Mr Smith over to him and hugged him in front of everyone. All of the children cheered again. Mr Smith was as respected and popular now as he ever was. Adam got down on his knees and bowed in front of him but Mr Smith just laughed and pulled him back to his feet.

Mr Smith took the opportunity to say a few words. He told the children that Adam was special because he had been given a rare talent by God but he told the children that what made Adam even more special was the way that he worked harder than any other boy he had taught before or since.

Adam had a surprise of his own for all of us. In recognition of Mr Smith's influence upon his life, Adam announced that he was setting up a bursary; a fund for gifted and talented children. It wasn't just for children of this school but for all the children of the community. It was not just for football either. It was for any child who showed promise in any sport. It was to be called the "Smith Award for Sporting Excellence". Mr Smith wasn't a man to wear his heart on his sleeve but it was clear that he was very moved by the gesture and the two men embraced again.

It was a very moving occasion. The children were clapping and cheering with enthusiasm. I stepped to the fore and gestured for them to be quiet for a while. A hush fell around the hall and I made another announcement. I said a few words of thanks to Adam on Mr Smith's behalf and I told him that his was not the final surprise because we had one more for him.

I told him that there was somebody else who had travelled a long way to see him today. I called to the back of the hall for him to come in. The children all clapped again because they knew who it was.

Then another hush fell about the room as a solitary figure approached.

Adam's father walked slowly into the hall on his own two feet without the aid of crutches or sticks.

Adam called out, "Dad! Dad!"

He jumped from the stage and ran down to him. He had never been able to make himself truly believe that he would ever see this day.

He told me later that it felt as though he had looked upon the face of God.

We all have talent. The lucky ones know it.

## Epilogue

*It was a shame to have to change the names of the characters and clubs involved in this story but it would have been unfair to have written so candidly about Adam's unhappy childhood. It would have been very unfair to blacken the names of good footballing clubs because of wrong doing in the past. Illegal payments were rife in the game back then and so it would be unfair to bring the attention of one to the public when so many of them were guilty of the same practices.*

*I felt that this story needed to be told. Ever since the first people ever walked upon this earth, men and women have struggled to make the best of their lives. This was a story of struggle. It was a struggle that started at a very early age. Adam had to hide his dreams and keep them locked up in a diary. I hope that this story will inspire young people who read it to be proud of their dreams. I hope that young people who read this story will work hard to keep their dreams alive. That is the important thing. Struggle is important because life is tame and dull without it.*

This book has been a success if you resolve to keep your dream alive forever.